Praise for
Rejection Letters

Who knew anyone could make rejection so appealing? You won't be able to suppress a wry smile or even a guffaw as you read through the riotous reasons these cantankerous editors find to dis these hopeful Heaneys.

~ Tanya Farrelly, author of *The Girl Behind the Lens*
    and *When Black Dogs Sing*

The writer's greatest enemy is the unsympathetic editor and the rejection letter. And in the Irish magical and poetry traditions the most effective weapon to destroy your enemy is satire. So, just as the sixth-century Irish poet Seanchán Torpest is said to have killed ten mice stone dead with a poem, Edward O'Dwyer's *Rejection Letters* is his dark and humorous defence against the powers of rejectomancy. This collection is the perfect charm against any editor's No.

~ John W. Sexton, author of *Futures Pass* and
    The Offspring of the Moon

As an editor of 43 years standing, I find it comforting that you trust me to comment on your most recent work. Yes, it does connect closely to my own deep and pointless ponderings over the years. Poets, as you know, are born, not made, and it is good that they have a kick up the backside every now and then to keep them to their true calling. With that in mind, I heartily endorse your book of said kickings, and, it must be said, acknowledge the truth therein.

~ Jessie Lendennie, editor, *Salmon Poetry*

REJECTION LETTERS

EDWARD O'DWYER

TRUTH SERUM PRESS

ISBN: 978-1-923000-78-0

BP#00134

Truth Serum Press
32 Meredith Street
Sefton Park SA 5083
Australia

Email: truthserumpress@live.com.au
Website: truthserumpress.net
Truth Serum Press catalogue: truthserumpress.net/catalogue

Original free cover photograph copyright © Lucas George Wendt
Author photo by Niall Hartnett
Cover design copyright © Matt Potter

Also available as an ePub eBook
ISBN: 978-1-923000-94-0
Also available as a Kindle eBook
ISBN: 978-1-923000-98-8

Truth Serum Press is a member of the
Bequem Publishing collective

www.bequempublishing.com

for all the poetry editors
who give up their time and energy
often without thanks

Also by Edward O'Dwyer

The Rain on Cruise's Street
Salmon Poetry, 2014

Bad News, Good News, Bad News
Salmon Poetry, 2017

Cheat Sheets
Truth Serum Press, 2018

Exquisite Prisons
Salmon Poetry, 2022

The Man Who Became Poems
Limerick Writers' Centre, 2023

An Introduction

This book contains 100 letters by fictitious poetry editors to fictitious poets turning down, for varying reasons, their fictitious poetry submissions. It examines the poet/editor relationship through a darkly comic lens and, hopefully, reveals much truth in all its exaggerated humour, which there is plenty of.

You don't need to be a poet or an editor to enjoy the book or to 'get' all the jokes – far from it! – but those who are one or the other or even both will be able to relate to so much of this. The relationship between poet and editor is usually polite and dull on the surface but this book turns it into the soap opera it could be. How? These fictitious editors don't hold back.

The rejection the poet suffers is not unique. Precious creatures that they are, they like to think it is special, a pain that strikes a place of depth 'regular people' just don't possess. It's not the case. The rejection they deal with is just very specific, that's all.

I don't want to diminish it, however – it can hurt. The nature of rejection will always be that it has that possibility of inflicting a pain, and we all have the wounds of rejection to some degree, whether it was someone who didn't want to go out with you when you were teenagers, a job you applied for only to be snubbed, or maybe a doorman at a nightclub who just said 'Not tonight' after a cursory glance at you, offering no constructive feedback you might take on board for the next time.

Poets write the best poems they can, then send them to a journal that publishes poems, and an editor there does or doesn't publish them. That's the process at its most basic, the frills removed.

The poet, learning the outcome, rejoices or sulks, brags or whinges. You can try to reduce your encounters with it, but it is unlikely poets will avoid rejection entirely.

When they start sending poems out for publication, most of these would-be poets learn it is inevitable to receive rejection letters. They seem as sure as rain and taxes. In most cases they're generic, bland and polite to the point of nauseating. There is even a stock of annoyingly inoffensive phrases and lines editors have assembled to avoid saying, simply, he/she disliked the poems.

Like that person who wouldn't go out with you all those years ago, and even like the doorman of that shit nightclub, you don't have to agree with any of these editors. You can believe they are wrong to refuse your poems, but they move on. Their inboxes fill up again faster than they can empty them, and poets need to move on as well, accept their decisions, and not send the same poems the next time they try to convince those editors to publish their poems. You can take the rejection any way you want to. Continue to believe the poems perfect, send them elsewhere. You can review them, too – see if there's anything you can improve on. Was there a glaring typo that entirely dampened their effect?

I could spend all day writing about rejection in the context of sending poetry submissions out to poetry journals, but I won't do that since I'm trying to convince you to read the book, not bury it deep in the back garden. I just want to explain briefly how the idea for the book came about.

I saw a Facebook post recently about whether sending out submissions is worth it at all, and it got me thinking. I don't do much of it anymore, and I hadn't ever really wondered why.

The subject of the post was the amount of time and effort it took to prepare a submission, as was how much doing so was a distraction from actual writing. I think these are fair points but the poet who posted on Facebook is well-known already and that matters here.

The other subject of the Facebook post concerned the replies poets can receive from editors, bemoaning how the already long-suffering poet might wait months upon months for an answer. The poet might never receive a reply, even, and still wonder on their death bed if the magazine received their submission.

The poet might also get a 'thanks but no thanks' form reply, a copy and paste effort. For this, there is likely a curtly dismissive letter, but worse again is its overcompensating Other, the heavily platitude-stocked version.

Finally, the poet might receive a borderline rude reply amounting to a dressed-up 'fuck off' from the editor. It is these this book is most interested in.

There's nothing quite like a memorable rejection letter. It can feel great. It might be rude, and it might be just plain bizarre, but I think any writer would say these are much better than the excruciatingly bland diplomacy of 'your work is not a good fit for us at this time'. Those tend to make me sorry I bothered, but a rude one? Yes, please!

Now, what if the rude and bizarre were not the exception but the norm? This book imagines a poetic world where this is the case. It dreams up the rude, the wild, the mad, and the petty letters that might have been. They are the rejections I'd love to tell other writers of, boast of. I wouldn't like to be on the receiving end of all of them, but definitely a few.

Today is the first of August. It is hot, steamy and wet. It is raining. I am tempted to write a poem. But I remember what it said on one rejection slip: 'After a heavy rainfall, poems titled 'Rain' pour in from across the nation.'

Sylvia Plath

Dear Mr. Simmons,

Thank you for sending your poems to us for consideration.

I'll thank you not to send them to us ever again.

Sincerely,

Blake Hindley, Editor-in-Chief.

The Altruist Poetry Journal

Dear Ms. Brannigan,

It's a 'no' from us on this occasion, but you shouldn't take it as a negative reflection on your work, the quality of which, at this time, I'd feel unable to comment on with any degree of fairness.

I have a devastating hangover, you see, and on these days the answering of submissions to *Orbital* does tend to be a bit like Russian Roulette where the gun always contains six bullets rather than one.

Do feel free to send poems to us again, and if you do, maybe (with any luck) I won't be so under the weather.

Yours sincerely,

Adam O'Shaughnessy, Poetry Editor and Web Design.

Dear Mr. Bennis,

I'll have to pass on these poems, but I do thank you heartily for sending them to us at *Dragon's Lair*.

I must pass on the basis that I once dated a man with the same name as you and was so mercilessly rejected by him that to this day there remains a sucking wound where once was my heart, and I thought it might do it and me some good to reject you.

If you've ever written a poem for cathartic reasons, then maybe you will understand my logic here.

I do hope you understand, and if you do, you may also understand – and not take it too personally – when I suggest you perish brutally in a hit-and-run by a combine harvester.

Regretfully (not),

Jane Feldman, Associate Editor.

Dear Ms. Flowers,

I was about to send you an acceptance for two of the poems to be published in the next issue of *Orchid Fever*, but I've changed my mind. Why, you may wonder – more on a whim than anything else.

I understand you might be disappointed by this. It's not easy to be rejected, but tougher again to come so close, but then it's these letters that I love sending the most.

With every best wish,

Wendy Devine, Staff Editor.

Dear Ms. Epstein,

I'm conscious of the possibility that telling you how I really feel about the poems you sent to us at *Harlot Queen* might cause you to suffer a nervous breakdown, and so instead I'll just say no, we won't be publishing them.

As you process this knock to your confidence, please try to keep in mind that this process is a highly subjective one, and that there are probably editors out there who may actually want to publish this standard of work. Stranger things do happen.

Kind Regards,

Wanda Mulligan, Magazine Director.

Dear Mr. Lennon,

We are currently not considering poems composed of more emojis than words, but I do salute your efforts to be edgy and contemporary.

I would also point out that we've updated our submission guidelines to be clearer about this so you can decide more efficiently the next time if your poems will be a good fit here.

With thanks,

Jeremy Heinz, Poetry and Reviews Editor.

The Ventriloquist's Apprentice

Dear Mr. Higgins,

There are hundreds of reasons why I couldn't take these poems for publication here at *Centurion Magazine.*

My intern will be in touch soon with the full list. I would urge you to consider this full list of reasons before you feel encouraged to send more poems to us.

I won't say anything as trite as I look forward to reading more of your work.

Commiserations,

Leah French, Staff Editor and Accounts.

Dear Mr. O'Kane,

We were very sorry to hear about the death of your parents, and in such a freak tragedy, too. There was a sense, however, that mentioning this more than once in your cover letter was an attempt at coercing us into an emotional decision.

We, as editors of *Bequeathed Literary Journal*, feel the pangs of grief as much as the next person, but poems must be judged on their literary merit, and that alone. This has always been the way of doing things at this reputable magazine.

We will not be publishing these poems, I'm sorry to say. We wish you the very best in your time of mourning. We hope the rejection suffered here will not add to your already considerable pain, but I'd be sure enough your parents would not be thrilled at you attempting to gain an advantage in the poetry world from the circumstances of their untimely demise.

Deepest sympathies,

Edgar Roberts, Editor and Marketing.

Dear Mr. Owens,

Your submission did not state belonging to at least four different minorities, and so I must turn down these poems. There is a checklist of minority categories in our online submissions manager which you have left blank.

If you do meet the requirements for inclusion, then you may send them to us again, but I doubt you do because I read the poems, and they just seem a bit too smug and privileged in both their tone and subject.

Yours sincerely,

Linda Whyte, Poetry and Letters Editor.

Exclusion Zone

Dear Ms. Walters,

I wept openly and copiously while reading your work, and I don't mind admitting it.

It didn't move me, though. It was nothing like that. I think it was the state of poetry I wept for when I was reading your efforts. I think it was the loss of my youth to reading such submissions that I wept for. I can hardly count the years I've been doing this. I wish those sending poems would think about that sometimes, but I expect they never will.

I do have one suggestion. You might consider writing your poems on napkins in the future, so that editors such as myself might use them to catch the tears that may, from time to time, run down our cheeks.

Tearfully,

Benjamin Groot, Chief Editor.

Perplexity

Dear Mr. Bond,

While technically-speaking there is much to admire in the six poems you have sent me, I'll have to turn them down, I'm afraid.

If you'd sent me two or three about sex, then this might have contained better news, but six poems about sex! You've made your point! You're having it. Good for you! I, on the other hand, haven't got laid in twenty-three years. I'm sad to say that 'I'm a poetry editor' isn't the panty-twitching line that it once was.

I'm going to reject you now simply because a little rejection might do you some good. I understand hearing 'no' is beneficial to us all in moderation.

I'd wish you well now in your future endeavours, but it hardly seems necessary.

Yours enviously,

Adrian Costello, Editor and Social Media Manager.

Lost Realm

Dear Ms. Flores,

One of the beautiful things about poetry – and it might be the most beautiful thing about it – is how it changes and can constantly assume new shapes and ideas. Have you noticed how it reinvents itself, all of the time?

Maybe in the future, poetry will change into something akin to what you do in your writing, but until it does, I'm afraid I'll not be able to publish these gallant tries.

I would add that, while I greatly appreciate poetry's capacity to 'grow' and develop, I do not believe that every possible change is to be considered growth.

Every good wish,

Katya Holland, Creative Director.

Clinical View

Dear Mr. Hawkins,

Allow me to spare your fragile ego the tedious platitudes of conventional editorship: no fucking way will I be publishing these.

Moodily yours,

Valory Krantz, Head of Poetry.

The Sentinel

Dear Ms. Frawley,

While I appreciate you sending these poems for consideration, they are not at this time a good fit for *Hermeneutic Energy*.

I don't expect there will ever be a time when such poems are a good fit here, but just in case, keep an eye on our submissions window, where we regularly update and refine the journal's objectives and preferences, especially for our sporadic themed issues. Perhaps there could be one on the theme of grief, since my funeral would, I expect, come in close proximity to these developments.

Mournfully,

Evelyn Harnett, Poetry and Photography.

Dear Mr. Reynolds,

I read the pages you've sent with great interest. I laughed heartily, in fact. My sides and my jaw ached from the laughing I did while reading them. It was only on the second reading I realised humour is not at all what you were going for, which naturally changed completely my perception of the poems.

We'll not be able to publish them, but could they be altered or tweaked in some way to make comedy the intention? You should carefully consider this. I think there is a quick fix there for you to become a quite excellent poet from a rather passable one if you would go down that comedic route.

Uproariously yours,

Natasha Fitzroy, Poetry and Publicity Coordinator.

Manic Hibernation

Dear Ms. Livingstone,

I read your poems with interest, but I suspect you have misinterpreted the mission of *The Posthumist Magazine.*

We put this journal together to assemble and appreciate the wonderful poems that can become lost as a result of mortality. Even poets with twenty collections of poetry to their name are inevitably working on something new when they die, but where do those poems go? Who gets to read them? What great works have we lost this way? It is especially true today, with journals preferring to publish poets who are alive and active on social media.

While your poems are written from the point of view of being dead, it suggests a slight misconstruing of our name. I'm afraid that our periodical exists to bring together the living voices of those who have passed on. You may correct me if I am mistaken, but I have the impression you are, in fact, still very much alive.

It does state in our guidelines that the poems should be sent in by the departed's next of kin, with a copy of the death certificate in jpeg format, two conditions which are not met by your submission, and which give further reason to presume you are yet to shuffle off your mortal coil.

I can state that your poetry is sublime, and were you to suddenly pass away then I'd be delighted for your family to contact us with a view to bringing to life some of your unpublished works.

Until that time, or until a time we alter our submissions policy, I am unable to feature your poems in the magazine.

All best wishes,

Leon Helmsley, Editor-in-Chief.

Dear Ms. Murdoch,

We are so grateful that you have chosen to trust us with your poems here at *Eight Ball Says*. Thank you very much for sending them.

We asked the eight ball here in the office if we should publish them, and on this occasion the eight ball has declined.

Yes, we do actually make these tough decisions with an eight ball.

That way they're not so tough and, as a team of editors, we never have to get into a row or give any explanation about why we do and don't publish certain works.

In the eight ball we trust!

We wish you the best of luck in placing these poems elsewhere and hope you'll send us more of your work in the future, where we'll give it no consideration again, and instead simply ask the eight ball.

Due to a high volume of submissions here, we do ask that you wait three months from this date before submitting again.

With best wishes,

Randolph Hession, Associate Eight Ball Shaker.

Dear Ms. Bailey,

My intern, who sorts through our piles of submissions, placed your poems on my desk, something I hope will comfort you to some degree.

At a poetry press we are usually very grateful to our interns. What they lack in experience they make up for in enthusiasm, sucking up, and free labour verging on exploitation. We work on small budgets, as you'll surely know, and we can't turn down free help.

I've never actually fired an intern before, but it looks as though I'll have to fire this one.

Yours sincerely,

Beverly Cannon, Digital Media and Poetry Editor.

Bad Habitat

Dear Ms. Jenkins,

Allow me to get straight to the point here: I'm getting screwed in alimony and I'm beginning to experience difficulties achieving an erection.

Ordinarily these things would have nothing to do with your submission of poems to *Opposing Instincts*, but today I feel like taking my personal laments out on somebody, and outside of this editorship I have little to no power or influence upon the world, so it'll just have to be you, I'm afraid, who I take my problems out on.

I certainly hope you're feeling quite pleased with yourself about all of this.

Dejectedly,

Grant Anderson, Poetry and Translations Editor.

Dear Mr. Allenby,

I love poetry, and as much as that, I love chocolate. Since you didn't send me anything that resembles poetry, I'll just have to thank you for the smudge of chocolate on one of the pages. I licked it clean, and it was quite delicious.

As I'm sure you've already been able to determine, the poems will not feature in *This Ability Magazine*.

Yours decadently,

Sharon Davidson, Reviews and Poetry.

Dear Ms. Avery,

I regret that I am not in a position to give you comprehensive feedback on your submission of poems to *Lucid Psychosis*, but if we were ever to publish a poem that was sent in scrawled crudely in pink crayon, it really would need to be something very special indeed.

We wish you the very best in your writing endeavours, whichever colours they may be in.

Kindest regards,

Graham Smith, Poetry Editor and Assistant Fiction Editor.

Dear Ms. Bryce,

I'm a lover of poetry and boxes of chocolates, and always find that being sent poems by somebody you haven't come by previously is little different to selecting a piece from a box of chocolates that's new to you also.

As Forrest Gump said, you just don't know what you're going to get. You bite into it and it might be ecstasy, pure nirvana.

Once or twice, though, you bite into it and the taste is so disagreeable you retch and spit the contents of your mouth across the room.

I'm afraid your poems fell into the second category. I will know the next time I see your name appear in the submissions not to be so recklessly enthusiastic.

If it consoles you at all, many chocolatiers seem to persist with those horrid, vomit-inducing additions to their otherwise wonderful produce, which convinces me that somebody is eating them and, by the same token, it might offer you reassurance that somebody out there will want to publish your poems.

Nauseously,

Dexter Earnshaw, Managing Editor.

Camomiles To Go

REJECTED

Dear Mr. Hastings,

I'm not sure why you sent your poems to *The Pick-Pocket Poet*. We only publish poets from disadvantaged backgrounds. This is stated very clearly in our guidelines.

It seems to me you just wanted to brag about your fancy degrees, your M.A. this and your PhD that. Am I right?

Well, I don't give a fuck how educated you are. You ain't shit to me. Your bio note mentions reciting poetry to royalty all over the world. If that's meant to impress me, let me tell you, it makes me sick.

Our contributors don't need any of those parchments on the walls. They write poetry from the heart. They write it in blood with their bleeding fingertips.

Go have yourself some afternoon tea and leave the poetry to us.

Just in case I haven't been clear, we must decline publishing your poems as your submission doesn't meet the criteria set out in the journal's mission statement.

Keeping it real,

Brian Simmons, Poetry Editor.

Dear Mr. Ranier,

While your poems certainly took me on a journey I'll not soon forget, I'll not be able to publish them in *Sprightly Muse.*

Your poems brought me to places I'm stronger for having been, I'm sure, but if it can be helped at all, I won't ever go back.

Please do me the kindness of waiting until next year to send poems again, when I'll have completed my stint as editor of this fine journal.

Yours gratefully,

Aaron Winterson, Guest Editor.

Dear Mr. Ellery,

I counted the words in your biographic note, and it exceeds the fifty permitted by a full three words.

For that reason we are disqualifying your poems from consideration at *Inert Soul* and suggest you trim down that biographic note if you'd like to be published by us in the future. I mean, who do you think you are?

Yours considerately,

Angela Ackerman, Prose and Poetry Editor.

Dear Mr. Hendrick,

Thank you, of course, for sending your poems to us here at *Whittle*, but thank you most of all for printing your poems on such an exceptional quality of paper. When I wiped my backside with them it chafed only minimally.

I haven't had to purchase toilet roll in years. There are always submissions like yours coming in, and as long as I preside here as editor, I'll probably not be buying any. You see, I was never comfortable buying it at the supermarket. I always felt the store clerk's judgement when I did, like I was a let-down to the human race just because I needed to wipe my posterior from time to time.

Anyway, I wanted to respond to your submission as a courtesy. I was raised with the ideal that one courtesy should breed another, and so forth, and so forth.

With every best wish,

Samuel Bottoms, Poetry Editor.

Dear Mr. Bloom,

We've decided, after giving it careful consideration, to make *Steamy Cauldron* a journal for women only.

Please don't take it as any reflection of the quality of your poems, as it is for purely biological reasons that we must on this occasion say no.

If you decide to undergo any major identity reevaluation in the future and then deem yourself eligible to submit once more, please do send us a query.

Graciously,

Gloria Babcock, Translations and Poetry Editor.

Dear Ms. Dylan,

I shouldn't be responding to submissions while stupefied drunk, but sometimes the liquor takes the edge off.

Anyway, I've managed to knock over a bottle of red wine across your poems, and I just can't determine if they are any good or not, or a fit in terms of style for *Vagrant Mist.*

I will, of course, be unable to include any of them now. You'll be disappointed, I'm sure, but not disheartened, I hope, and I trust this episode won't deter you from sending us your work again in the future.

You could even resend the same stuff, since I haven't been able to reject it on the grounds of quality, and I wouldn't even know that you'd sent it in previously.

Imagine me in my office, desperately trying to lick red wine up off the pages, just enough to make out something of the poems.

You may – and I hope you do – observe some dedication and commitment in this effort to salvage the work, and please understand that the situation is deeply regretted by me, and in the spirit of cultivating a good relationship, I'm enclosing a copy of two of our back issues with this letter.

Rather drunkenly,

Gavin Warnock, Poetry Editor and Media Manager.

Dear Ms. Fennessy,

Today I'm flipping a coin, so the good news is that every submission of poems to *Dancing Star* has a 50% probability of success. I'm sure my mathematics is wrong, of course. It usually is.

I have already accepted much lacklustre work today – the coin's choice, not mine. Your technically flawless and rather original poems did not make the cut this time round. Still, ordinarily our acceptance rate is less than 2%, owing to the high volume of submissions we receive, and if I'm honest, we do solicit work from friends and benefactors as well, so I'm sure you'll be most grateful to have had your best chance of publication in our esteemed magazine.

Lazily yours,

Becka Friel, Poetry Editor and Production Manager.

Dear Mr. Durst,

There are rules. Namely, you must subscribe to the journal for a minimum of a year before sending me your poems for possible inclusion in its pages.

It is standard practice here to consider poems only by poets who keep us financially afloat. This is a practice we were compelled to introduce a few years ago, when we noticed there were a lot of submissions coming in but not so many subscriptions.

We look forward to receiving your subscription and, naturally, in due course, your poems.

The coming year as a subscriber will give you a great opportunity, I'm sure, to acquaint yourself with the kind of work we tend to publish, which you did not manage to send this time.

Yours expectantly,

Sarah Silverstein, Publicist and Editor.

The Garden Party

Dear Mr. Pierce,

I was just thinking that reading your submission of poems had been entirely wasteful on my part when, suddenly, the dog peed on the kitchen linoleum. I knew I was out of used newspapers so I became very grateful to have your poems to hand and no other positive to make of their existence.

I was anything but absorbed in the reading of them, but am pleased to tell you they were most absorbing in at least one sense of the word.

If you ever send poems again to *Vague Apparition* then I'll hope for the same timeliness. Sable is a good dog, but she is getting on in years and the bladder control just isn't the sealed vault that it once was.

Gratefully,

Jeannette Peabody, Web Design and Poetry Reader.

Dear Ms. Morrow,

I was thinking I might include one or two of the poems from your submission in the next issue of *Obtuse Angles*, and then I remembered you served as editor of an anthology called *Embittered Heart* a few years back, an anthology to which I sent some poems that received a maddeningly lukewarm response.

Admittedly it is somewhat petty of me, but since you didn't publish mine, I've decided not to publish yours. The wheel turns, as you can see.

I'm also serving on the judging panel for the *Poison Darts Prize* this year and will keep an eye peeled for your entry.

Vengefully yours,

Patrick Briscoe, Poetry Editor and Events Coordination.

Dear Mr. Eggers,

These poems you've sent in are immensely dark and perhaps the bleakest snapshot of internal struggle that I've encountered in my decades as a poetry journal editor, and I don't mean it in the good way. In fact, I very much fear that you are on the brink of taking your own life, and certainly hope I am mistaken.

I cannot, however, print this work on the basis that it might give your self-esteem a much-needed boost. Sadly, I must think of the integrity and reputation of the journal and put sentiment to one side. I must judge all pieces solely on their literary merits and be swayed by nothing, which must even include compassion.

On this note, it is with great worry and concern that I must inform you that *Celluloid Sky* will not be including any of these poems in its next issue.

Extremely hopefully,

Deborah Bloom, Director and Editor.

Dear Mr. Wallin,

I was stung by a bee today, and it got me on the armpit, if you can believe that. It was a fine day and there haven't been many of those lately, so I thought I might read some of the submissions out in the garden, to enjoy a brief escape from the musty office. I even did up a batch of homemade lemonade to sip at.

I'll not be publishing any of the poems in your submission this time because I'm cranky and in pain and looking for someone to wound as some sort of relief to myself, and that someone is you. There will be others, if it helps you to know that.

No doubt you are smugly sting-free and taking it for granted but the sting of rejection is indeed headed your way.

Crankily,

Max Brennan, Reviews and Poetry Reader.

Alighting Softly

Dear Mr. Dugdale,

I must politely decline the opportunity to publish these poems which, if I'm being honest, I never did get around to reading.

I regret to say I found your cover letter just a bit too familiar, a bit too chummy. The tone left me questioning your understanding of the submission process. There is a professional distance and a formality that must be observed.

I would strongly advise against asking the editors of respected poetry journals you wish to be published in whether they'd like to meet up some time, and to perhaps get a drink or even sushi.

It's not that I didn't appreciate the offer, and I know a really good sushi place I've been meaning to return to. It's just that we take our professionalism very seriously here at *Soggy Sandwich*.

Suddenly rather hungrily,

Brett McIntosh, Editor and Sales.

Dear Ms. Hilton,

I do love it when I receive work of the calibre of Frost or Heaney or Bishop. It's why I do what I do.

Wading, and indeed trudging through submissions like yours is a necessary part of that journey. We must kiss many frogs before our prince reveals himself.

Your poems will not be featured in *Crooked Moon*, but please take heart from knowing that your attention to and execution of formatting particulars was first rate.

With all good wishes,

Jessica Ford, Managing Editor and Reviews Commissioner.

Dear Ms. Irving,

Thank you for giving me the opportunity to read these. We are always grateful for the trust you offer when you send poems our way.

We'll have to decline them, however, and while I can't offer in-depth feedback on any submission, it would be remiss of me not to point out that you are not e.e. cummings, so do the poetry world and yourself a favour and start using capital letters.

It doesn't mean that you will have poems published by *Lapsed Intent* in the future, but I expect you'll have improved your chances a great deal.

If you'd like in-depth feedback on any submission, there is a purchase option for that on our website under 'Shop' in our drop-down menu.

Yours sincerely,

Freddie Grayson, Reviews and Poetry Associate.

Dear Mr. Phillips,

I've misplaced my glasses and you've sent in poems in the smallest print I've ever had to read in all my years as an editor. I've a pain in my head now after squinting through them, a pain so great I don't even care anymore if they are worth publishing or not, and I'm just going to say no fucking way.

Begrudgingly,

Dwayne Leonard, Assistant Poetry and Letters Editor.

Rusty Musket

Dear Ms. Geary,

It's been such a cold winter, and with rises in fuel prices and everything else, I've fallen behind in the payment of my heating bill and have resorted to burning poetry submissions faster than I've been able to read them. Thank goodness we are so established here at *Sudden Thought Syndrome* and therefore receive a high volume of submissions from a global scribbling population.

I didn't get to read yours, so I can't possibly include them in an edition now, but please send more soon, very soon, while also understanding that I'm behind, too, on my electricity bill and there's only so much natural light in these dark and oppressive days.

Warmest wishes,

Bernard Linnane, Editor-in-Chief.

Dear Mr. Conroy,

Thank you for sending poems to *Gelatin Cloud*, but we have decided we cannot process them any further as they fail to comply with submission standards.

Had you taken the care to adhere to these standards, you would have included the comma between your last name and 'Poetry' in the subject line of your email. Instead, you have very recklessly used a semi-colon.

If you do not take this journal seriously in your submission, then I'm sure you don't expect us to take the submission seriously either. These standards are specified for a reason, and disregard of them will always lead to your poems remaining unread, and instead of news of publication you can expect a mildly scolding email like this one.

Rather huffily,

Barbara Hirsch, Layout Design and Poetry Reader.

Dear Ms. Wilson,

I'm informing all would-be contributors to *Quillity* that I've suffered a terrible car accident that has left me with partial amnesia. It's an awful and quite unusual inconvenience. I forget everything I once knew about poetry and seem to be able to remember everything else. Now, when I read submissions to the magazine, I genuinely can't tell if they're any good or not.

To avoid damaging the esteemed reputation the magazine has built and continues to build since its inception, I've decided it best to decline all poetry sent in, effective now and until further notice.

I have made commitments to publish work prior to my injury, which I trust was made with access to full and ample faculties, and so publishing this work will go ahead as planned and will take us through the next two issues.

I hope to have full restoration of my faculties by then and will include updates on my condition in our monthly newsletter, which you might consider subscribing to now if you have not already done so.

I regret any inconvenience caused to you, but I'm sure you can appreciate my acting in the best interests of the journal. You sent your work to the very best, no doubt, because you wish it to share a space with the very best, and I intend for that to be the case.

Forgetfully yours,

Harriet Bell, Poetry Editor.

Dear Ms. Withers,

I suspect you copied and pasted your cover letter, and I suspect this because you got the name of our journal wrong.

I could forgive this in most cases.

I know what it's like when you're sending out submissions and taking time from your busy day. I'm not without compassion here.

However, you sent the poems first to our bitterest rival. That makes it a rather different matter.

If I may use a euphemism, we hate them. They get more funding than us, and for what? They only produce two issues per year. I'm sure you sent to them first because of the larger contributor fee they can offer, but payment is not everything, something all poets should know very well.

I wish you luck with your submission to them. We'll not be considering your poems any further here at *Violet & Indigo,* not now, and don't be at all surprised if we hold a grudge.

Somewhat bitterly,

Rachel Vickers, Magazine Director.

Dear Mr. Spalding,

Our guidelines clearly state poems should be no more than fifty lines long, and that includes blank lines.

This is for formatting reasons, and so that we can maximise the number of contributions to the magazine. It is up to you to count the lines in your poems.

Our intern has alerted me to the fact that one of your poems has four extra lines.

Either you did not put the required care into your submission, or you decided your poems deserved special treatment, but whichever it is, we have standards to uphold here at *Nettle Soup*, which is why we will go ahead with publication of that poem but have removed the final four lines.

What do you think of that, eh?

You probably think those lines are crucial to the meaning and effect of the poem, and that's what we're counting on.

None of us should get to thinking we are more important than other contributors, I'm sure you'll agree.

Yours sincerely,

Carol Fairgreen, Poetry Associate and Digital Development.

Dear Mr. Joyce,

I'm not sure selecting random paragraphs from *Finnegan's Wake* and adding line breaks to them is what we're looking to publish here at *Mercury Rising*. I'm not sure it qualifies as original poetry.

You've given them rather apt titles, and they do seem to work on some level as poems (they scan well), but I have concerns around the issues of copyright and intellectual theft. In this regard, I'm sure you'll be helped out somewhat by the coincidence that your name happens to also be James Joyce, but even still, I'll have to err on the side of caution and decline them.

Bemusedly,

Finbar Whitely, Managing Director.

Dear Ms. Horgan,

Sometimes, as an editor of a poetry journal, you just want to be sent work in which the words are all spelled correctly, with punctuation marks appearing in the correct places, and that will be enough to be published.

You were doing so well in your submission of poems to *Teacup Typhoon.* You very nearly made it to the end.

Kindest wishes,

Melanie Bradshaw, Poetry and Prose Reader.

Dear Mr. Carson,

As a vegan poetry journal which specialises exclusively in vegan ideas and experiences and expressions, I find your poems barbaric and upsetting, and I can't help wondering if you've sent them to us in order to be deliberately provocative. I mean really, how many innocent animals must be slaughtered and eaten just so you can write a poem?

Disgustedly yours,

Mia Grady, Editor and Vegan Correspondent.

Green Streets

Dear Mr. Wood,

I regret to say that I cannot give you special treatment just because you're my father, and even if you have paid for my education, which you have strategically reminded me of in your cover letter, but from all here at *Chocolate Muse*, we're glad you've found a hobby, and we wish you the very best in your retirement.

Keep developing your craft and we'll be delighted to read some more of your poems in the future.

Every best wish,

Gavin Wood, Poetry and Commercial Director.

Dear Mr. Watkins,

Thank you for sending us poems for consideration but don't send us anymore, please.

Poetry may not be your strong suit, but did you ever consider applying to the C.I.A.? Sometimes you'd hear about them having to torture prisoners for information, and I don't mind telling you, thirty seconds of listening to these and I'd be ready to talk. I'd tell you everything I knew, no matter the cost to myself, my family, my country. I'm quite sure I'd just want the pain to stop.

In agony,

Darren Fielding, Chief Poetry Editor.

Rebuttal Magazine

Dear Mr. Moran,

The technical quality of poetry is, in my expert opinion, going down. Quite steadily, I've noticed it dropping, plummeting, in fact, and we have had to publish inferior stuff as a result.

I can't publish these right now here at *Lambent Flame*, but if my calculations are correct, they'll likely be sought after in approximately 200 years, and the editors (I'll be dead), I expect, will be most grateful to receive them.

Faithfully yours,

Yvonne Kelkin, Editor-in-Chief.

Dear Mr. Fagan,

Thank you for sending your poems to *Serpent Skin*. We gave them due consideration before taking the decision not to publish them.

In the most recent update to our submission guidelines, we requested quite clearly that all submissions be sprayed with a pleasing perfume or cologne. One or two sprays would be sufficient. There is no need to drench the pages. It is not mandatory, but you may also mention in your cover letter which fragrance you use.

We noticed around the office that the build-up of stacks of paper can produce a rather stale and pungent smell, and this was the solution we agreed upon. The office has been smelling wonderfully ever since.

Having neglected to follow this prerequisite to submission, I couldn't consider the poems on their literary merits. It is vital that you check and adhere to the guidelines as they are regularly reviewed. Sometimes we even throw in some irrelevant tweaks, just to catch people out and whittle down the volume of submissions. When you think you know our guidelines very well, that's when we'll look to pull the rug out from under you. I hope this is helpful ahead of your next submission.

Yours sincerely,

Melinda Verhoeven, Photography and Poetry Editor.

Dear Ms. Farrelly,

Thank you for your interest in *Bouquet Literary Journal* and also thanks for the opportunity to read your poems.

I regret to say we won't be able to use these. Each one is basically a rewrite of Wordsworth's 'Daffodils', just changing the name of the flower and, where necessary, some of the imagistic details. Of course, I'm sure you know this and it was probably what you were going for.

I did enjoy reading them, I'll admit, even if they are painfully derivative and lacking in originality. I've always been very fond of Wordsworth's better stuff.

Kindest regards,

Hank Grealish, Managing Editor and Web Designer.

Dear Ms. Holly,

Thank you for the brevity of your poems. It is their best asset.

Good luck with placing them elsewhere, whether it be the bin, the shredder or the fireplace.

Kind regards,

Mavis Bierce, Reviews and Poetry Associate.

Genus

Dear Mr. Durack,

I know our mission statement encourages new writers to send work to us, but that's because we find they are more likely to be persuaded to take out a subscription rather than any sincere desire to publish their half-baked musings.

I'm delighted to see from our records that you have indeed bought a subscription, but I'm sorry to say that I'll not be publishing the poems you submitted because I've never heard of you.

Yours bluntly,

Caleb Finnegan, Editor and Publicist.

The Conceit Review

Dear Ms. Quaid,

My hair hasn't cooperated at all this week. It happens sometimes, but when it does, the acceptance rate here at *Highway Surf* certainly nosedives. Is there a connection between the two things? Oh, I'd say so.

On a better hair week, I think I'd have used two of these poems. Maybe that's comforting to you, or maybe it's more frustrating. I don't particularly care at this moment.

Keep an eye out for our upcoming newsletter, where we'll be announcing the theme for an anthology marking twenty-five years publishing the finest contemporary poetry from around the world. Perhaps better hair days are ahead for me, which might mean good things for your submission.

Sincerely,

Irene Sweeney, Poetry Editor.

Dear Mr. Bonner,

I admire the balls it must have taken to send these poems to *Elite Magazine*. Everyone at the office has been very impressed all morning (by your balls, not your poetry), and I mean that quite genuinely.

Unfortunately, in terms of your submission, it takes much more than balls to be published by us, so we are declining these. We have, however, put one of them up on the door of the office fridge as a sort of wellbeing in the workplace initiative. I hope that's okay with you.

Admiringly,

Avril Newell, Director and Editor.

Dear Ms. Hornby,

You spelled my name incorrectly, which means I took an instant dislike to your submission and hoped I'd find reasons to decline it. Sadly, I didn't find any clear and obvious reasons to say no, but then I realised it didn't really matter and I could just decline it anyway.

Yours powerfully,

Pepper Donoghue, Founder and Editor.

Gristle Papers

Dear Ms. O'Rahilly,

I was initially quite intrigued, impressed even, by the poems you sent in your submission to *Sentry Duty*. I was ready to publish them until I looked at your social followings. And thank goodness I did!

Networking is vital to what we do now, and we like to see that our contributors give time and effort to procuring a platform from which to promote themselves and, yes, us as publishers of their work.

The days of all that publicity falling entirely on the publisher are well and truly gone.

People can be no more sitting back on their laurels, especially poets.

It is rather arrogant of the modern poet to believe their job is only the writing of poetry, don't you agree?

You can be the most splendid tree in the forest, after all, but the readers are out on the roads and in their cars and whizzing by with places to be, and you must do something to convince them to pull over and walk into that deep, leafy place.

Proactively yours,

Ursula Bowen, Translations and Poetry.

Dear Ms. Mullins,

I'm grateful that you would send your poems to *Bone Structure* for consideration, but we'll not be able to publish them this time.

I'm sorry to be so blunt, but I really didn't have a notion what was going on in these. Perhaps they are works of great genius that I am unable, in my limitations, to appreciate. Perhaps they are not gibberish at all. Perhaps they are not trash heaps of words deposited on the page. Perhaps. Indeed.

Truly mystified,

Fredrick Winkel, Poetry Editor.

Dear Mr. Ashberry,

Thank you for submitting your poems to *Chimera's Revolt.*

While we do publish the occasional 'Shape Poem', I'm afraid these are not suitable to our needs, nor are they in line with our values.

A penis or two with some other shapes might have been somewhat acceptable, but five quite varied erect members suggests limitations in your poetic reach, while at this journal we are always striving for work with reach and heft, work that is wild and surprising yet at the same time poised.

Graciously,

Hilda Gibbons, Managing Editor.

Dear Mr. Kerrigan,

Thank you for trusting *Elliptic* with your poems, which we are always grateful to receive.

I wonder, though, was it intentional to submit them in all capital letters, or do you just need (but don't know how) to release the Caps Lock button on your keyboard? I didn't want to presume the answer, either way.

As it is, I found your submission difficult to assess within the fair process we pride ourselves on as a poetry journal. Your poetry came across as rather loud and intimidating. I felt shouted at as I tried to read them, and so struggled to enjoy them. My worry is that our readers might feel the same if we published them, and I'd worry for some of our more sensitive and vulnerable subscribers, and so I'll have to say no to them.

If it is a case that you were not sure how to release the Caps Lock button on your keyboard, I would happily invite you to resend these poems in the way you had intended, and I will look forward to reading them at their correct volume and tone.

Warmest wishes,

Gideon Payne, Assistant Editor.

Dear Mr. Goldman,

Here at *Damned Horoscope* we pride ourselves on our integrity, crucial to which is our policy of trust and honesty.

There is a lot I think another editor might admire in these poems, and I have every faith that they will be published in the future.

I, sadly, hate them. Even hate seems too small a word here. Despise? Detest? Poetry is just so personal and subjective, isn't it? I can't even say what it is I loathe about them.

I should be able to, but I can't.

I don't want to publish them. I think that must be clear enough. I'm quite sure after reading them that I never want to read another of your poems ever again.

Can I ask that you never again send any? It seems harsh to me, asking that, but I really would appreciate it.

I wish you the very best in placing these poems in another journal. If you do ever send poems here again, make sure they are your poems least like these ones.

Kindest regards,

Jacinta Murray, Editor-in-Chief.

Dear Ms. Linden,

Thank you, firstly, for your interest in *Cosmic Tango*, and may I say, your poems help us to keep this dance going.

This is the oddest thing. Your exact submission, word for word, was sent to me just yesterday. This could be a practical joke or a remarkable coincidence. I'm not able just yet to commit to a decisive response.

The other submission came from the other side of the world, it seems, and from somebody you have no links to on social media.

I checked, and there is no connection I'm able to discern. It really is quite bizarre, and I do enjoy a bit of the bizarre.

Down to the last comma, they are identical. Every line break is precisely the same.

Can there be unwitting plagiarism from thousands of miles away? And if there can, who is the plagiarist and the plagiarised? Yesterday I'd have said it was impossible, but today I am changed for the better, my mind blown open to an extraordinary degree.

Nevertheless, for legal reasons, I cannot publish either of you now.

With the utmost gratitude,

Lewis Rutherford, Editor and Marketing.

Dear Ms. Farrow,

Thank you for sending poems to *Delinquency*. Your cover letter mentioned they are 'Found Poems'. I'm curious, though, where did you find them, and was there any identifying information with them?

I loved them but couldn't possibly use them for publication under your name. If you found a manuscript by Chaucer, I'm sure you'd agree you'd not have the right to take it and publish it as yours, after all. Every effort must be made to locate the true author.

As it is, I'll be declining them. If you cannot identify who owns them, perhaps put them back where you found them, and maybe their owner will come back and check for them there.

Very best wishes,

Delia Edgeworth, Sales Executive and Poetry Reader.

Dear Mr. Whitely,

I enjoyed these poems quite a lot, but it has come to my attention that you once attended a neo-Nazi rally and were recorded reading poetry to the audience and then, later, taking part in the hate-fueled chants such parties tend to revel in.

Even if you have since seen the error of your ways, it would be problematic for us to publish your work in *Judge & Jewry*. We must think first of our reputation, and cannot risk upsetting valued contributors and subscribers.

Faithfully yours,

Corey Fleischer, Director and Public Relations.

Dear Ms. Lafferty,

We are so grateful to have received your submission to *Less is More Magazine*.

While it is certainly true that we do favour short and economical pieces, and so our name is to be factored in when sending work to us, it can, as it happens, be over-interpreted.

Your submission mentioned five poems, but you've only sent me five blank pages with your covering letter.

There is a point, it seems, at which less is not more, and it is, instead, not enough.

While I must turn down these poems (if that is what they are to be called), maybe you could send in their earlier drafts, before everything became over-edited, that is, if there were ever words in these poems to begin with.

I would add that I appreciate your respect for the mission of our magazine. So often we must turn down work that's too long, by poets who perhaps haven't bothered to read our mission statement and understand what we mean to do here.

Succinctly yours,

Philomena Belding, Poetry Reader and Cover Illustrator.

Dear Ms. Patterson,

This is going to sound ridiculous, I'm sure, but I am unable to process your submission of poems in the manner I would have liked, and in the manner to which we are accustomed here at *Hope Sachet.*

Did you ever have to tell a school teacher that your dog ate your homework? If you did, and it was true, then great, you will be able to appreciate what has happened.

Brandy Alexander isn't in the habit, however, of consuming poetry submissions. It is a first for her, and it makes me wonder if you might have been eating a sandwich at the time of preparing the poems, and if maybe a sliver of meat might have fallen out and onto the pages to leave a tempting smell behind on them.

Anyway, she ate them, and there's nothing much to be done about it.

If the poems reemerged on one of her trips out to the back garden, I'm sure they are entirely illegible now, so it isn't worth combing through each pile with aspirations of recovery.

If you'd care to send them in once more, I'll be sure to move your submission to the head of the line. We would hate to miss out on great poems, after all, and I accept that yours might have been just that.

Apologetically,

Benjamin Valverde, Chief Poetry Reader.

Dear Mr. Arthurs,

We pride ourselves foremost on our exceptional standard of elitism here at *Rented Skin*.

We can't say that in so many words in our submission guidelines, but did you not feel that it was implied?

Look at it this way; you have a rejection letter from us now, which is at least some acknowledgement that you exist, and perhaps more than you should have expected.

Maybe get a nice magnet and stick it up on the door of the fridge.

Dismissively yours,

Theodore Windsor, Poetry Editor.

Dear Ms. Holiday,

I hope you'll be quite pleased with yourself. The poems you sent in have blocked the toilet here at the office. Now there's shitty water all over the tiles and we've no mop. I'm about to head out to the shops to get one, and I'll have to dip into the subscriptions account for it, perhaps a plunger as well.

Obviously, we won't be publishing them, not after this. We politely decline, blah blah blah. Do you know how hard it is to even get a plumber on the phone, let alone get him to call by and do the job?

Oh yes, I hope you'll be very pleased indeed, and that you'll have a lovely little chuckle at our expense.

With contempt only,

Ernest Cleary, Poetry and Prose Editor.

Flush Review

Dear Mr. Garrett,

We read your poems with some interest but no more than that. They did have their merits, but it was your overly pompous and sanctimonious biographical note that led us to turn against them.

You certainly do know a great deal about congratulating yourself. We'll not be feeding that dangerously swelled ego, though, lest your head might burst. I'd feel for whoever might have to clean it up.

Listing out all your achievements is something we find very crass here. I'm sure there are journals who will be very impressed, and I suppose we wish you well placing your work with them, but things are done a little differently here at *Limping Cheetah*.

Unimpressed,

Belinda Graveson, Editor.

Dear Ms. Sheehan,

At first, I thought this was a poem called 'Shopping List'. After a while I realised it was your actual shopping list. I wonder if you were able to get fennel? I've had no joy finding it any time I've tried.

Anyway, goodness knows what you picked up at the supermarket when you got there, guided only by the poems you meant to send us.

For what it's worth, I was enjoying what I was reading quite thoroughly, and it was a certainty for publication until it became apparent that it wasn't the satiric commentary on modern living it first appeared.

Best wishes,

Colleen Kinder, Associate Editor.

Auntie Penultimate

Dear Ms. Deegan,

It isn't that we lack compassion for juvenile angst here at *Floating Anvil*. There is plenty of room in poetry for honest emotion.

The trouble for me, and the reason I'll have to pass on these poems, is they have a teenager's tendency toward nihilism, as well as a teenager's urgency of expression, and yet your biographical note mentions that you are a retired school teacher using poetry as a hobby to fill your time.

I suppose I expected poetry that was more reflective and ruminative in tone and subject. I must say I was bemused to encounter pages of trivial torment and images of hyperventilation.

While this is rejection, please consider it an opportunity to think about the kind of poet you want to be, and the kind of poet you should be. Perhaps ask yourself if you are being that poet.

If the answer is yes, then carry on doing what you are doing, and also never send work here again. If the answer, however, is no, then you must now figure out how to become this. It will not be simple, but the important poetry is always striven for. It is fought for, wrestled from the uncharted territories of the self.

I will look forward to hearing from that poet in the future.

Expectantly yours,

Derry Hobbins, Staff Editor and Graphic Design.

Dear Mr. Chesterfield,

We are pleased to have had the opportunity to read these poems but suspect you have written them all from the point of view of different varieties of fish.

They were interesting, especially the mortality-themed 'Canned', in which I felt a strong emotional connection to the tuna.

Still, it isn't quite what we are looking for here at *Gleaming Hook*.

Keep in mind for the future that our name is much more general than it perhaps seems. We have noticed a trend towards aquatics in submissions, and that is something we may need to address soon in the guidelines.

Anyway, we do wish you every success in your writing and would, as a courtesy, suggest the more niche and decidedly fish-themed *Seabed Junction* as a publisher for these.

I know the editor there and I think he'd enjoy them. He keeps an aquarium and regularly puts pictures of it on his social media.

Best wishes,

Janice Leamy, Poetry Reader.

Dear Mr. Floyd,

Thank you for your submission of poems. We read 'On Winning the Nobel Prize', 'On Winning the Pulitzer Prize' and 'On Winning the Griffin Poetry Prize' with great interest during our round-the-table sessions.

It is with regret, however, that we must refuse the opportunity to publish them. At *Alligator Tuxedo* we believe it is best to have won these awards before writing poems reflecting on the winning of them.

Should you ever win any of these awards, then – and I must stress only then – we would be happy to consider more of your work for publication.

Most sincerely,

Selena Braeburn, Head of Poetry and Translations.

Dear Ms. Bolinger,

We wish to inform you that your submission to *Green City Magazine*, while unsuccessful, was recycled appropriately and with respect for the environment.

This is paramount to our vision as a responsible poetry press. While you will be disappointed, at least your submission has not contributed to the undoing of poetry's future.

With our best wishes,

Melvin Greene, Staff Editor.

Dear Ms. Herring,

I'll get the formalities out of the way so I can get to the real business of my email: we will not be publishing these poems at *Secret Skin Poetry*.

As you may know, we don't usually respond to unsuccessful submissions, so you might be wondering why I'm contacting you now.

I am building up the courage to tell my parents that I'm gay, and since I had a rather conservative and small-minded upbringing, I expect they will not quite take it in their stride. It should come as no great surprise to them, but then one can never underestimate the power of denial, especially in backward communities like the one I left behind.

I figured I might begin building up the courage by telling some random strangers who are probably sensitive to alternative lifestyles. The writing of poetry, after all, is an alternative lifestyle in and of itself.

Yours was one of the drawn-at-random submissions I took from the stacks on my desk, and so there it is – I'm gay, and I have a boyfriend called Chip, and we live together with two cats called Lola and Phoebe.

Wait three months before sending your next submission, and thanks, of course, for your understanding.

Vulnerably,

Leon Waverley, Poetry and Reviews Manager.

Dear Mr. Beresford,

This, I suppose, is the part where the editor will usually thank you for the opportunity to read your poems, and if they do, it means they aren't going to publish them and probably wish you'd not sent them at all.

I'm not going to thank you because I don't mind telling you that I was not grateful at all for the opportunity to read your submission.

In fact, I'm deeply resentful and bitter to have read these poems, and to be left unable now to return to a time in my life and frame of mind when I hadn't read them, a time when poetry had a future, and a time when I might have stopped by a riverside to watch some ducks, or when I might have picked a flower and offered it to my wife, when I might have believed in the beauty and great purpose of small, earthly moments, but a time that is no more, alas, after having read your poems.

Ruefully yours,

Stephen Browning, Poetry Editor and Consultant.

The Hope User Manual

Dear Ms. Nickel,

We cannot say that our journal's 'tip jar' is mandatory. It simply wouldn't be in good taste, and we would likely come in for accusations of vanity publishing, I expect. We do very much consider ourselves a traditional press.

Still, the suggested donation also isn't as optional as it might appear. You see, I've only ever published work by people who put something in there.

Is that purely coincidental, do you think? Does it just so happen that theirs were the best poems every time?

I'll leave you decide that for yourself.

If you expect me to give up my time to reading your poems, then is it so much to ask that you'd buy me a coffee, or even a glass of wine?

Would it destroy your quality of life to do so? Would you be sleeping under a bridge as a result?

And so, we will not be publishing your poems this time around, but hope this email is helpful to you and your prospects of publishing work with us in the future.

Yours generously,

Ferdia Baxter, Director and Editor.

Formulae Review

Dear Mr. Lewisham,

I have read your poems many times over the course of some years and never come close to publishing any of them, and the result, this time, is the same.

I was more polite in the past, of course, but have had to make a few adjustments under the circumstances.

How long are we to go on in this way? If I ever said to you in our exchanges that I admire persistence, please allow me now to take it back.

Am I Sisyphus now, condemned forever to read these poems as some punishment by the gods? If so, I wish I knew my crime. Or is it you who is Sisyphus, condemned forever to send these submissions and to be told no, no, no and no?

Wearily yours,

Kendra Swift, Chief Poetry Editor.

Boulder Poet Magazine

Dear Mr. Fortune,

There are times in this job when it is best to be blunt.
These poems are about as useful to the world as the
audiobook of the *Kama Sutra*. Does it exist even?
I can't say with any certainty if it does or doesn't, but
I'd hope not.

There must be a better use for your stamps than
sending us your poems, and I'd urge you to find it.

Regards,

Carlton McKenzie, Poetry Editor.

Poetic Contortions

Dear Ms. Fleischer,

It is my duty to be honest and understanding and balance these things as best I can, a role I take very seriously indeed.

After all, at *Alloy Bones* we combine the highest standards of writing with nurturing the next generation of poets.

I can fondly remember my own first sojourn into the writing of poems, my unwavering expectation that they should be published, and my quiet confidence that the Nobel Prize would soon follow.

Let me tell you, I am grateful to the editors who brought me back down to Earth in their considerate rejections of my work. It was the platform upon which I was able to improve, being told 'no' back then, and so often.

I think your poems are about as bad as those poems I was writing, and I am hoping this rejection will benefit you now as theirs did me at that time.

You must remember each rejection is an opportunity, which makes me wonder, are there ever really any rejections?

Yours positively,

Edna Forestall, Managing Editor.

Dear Ms. Bartleby,

Let me begin by saying I am impressed by your creation of a whole new language, and your addition of dialectical variances and nuances to it. The problem is that I think our readers would feel aggrieved at reading such heavily footnoted work. In each outing, the footnotes are much longer than the poem itself.

Paralexical is, therefore, unable to publish your work this time, but we would suggest that you send in the English translations of these poems – if there are translations – and we would be very happy to consider them.

Kindest wishes,

Brandy Cafferty, Poetry Reader and Marketing Assistant.

Dear Mr. Valentin,

Every one of these so-called poems would make wonderful reading on the inside of a Hallmark card, and I don't mean that at all dismissively or patronisingly.

Sometimes the most important thing to know is who the most suitable publisher for our work is.

We couldn't possibly publish these at *Floating Candelabra,* but I would urge you to get in contact with the card companies, as they are always looking for new and fresh ways of communicating age-old sentiments.

With appreciation,

Gretchen Freund, Editorial Assistant.

Dear Ms. Warner,

By my records, this is the twenty-third time you have sent us your poems for consideration, and it is the twenty-third time *Cracked Vase* has turned them down.

That's correct, it's another no.

I've just done a quick count, and our relationship has had six anniversaries, would you believe?

We generally don't 'break up' with our would-be contributors, as poetry journals need submissions, but I really do think we need to talk.

I'm sure it's our loss, but your poems are just not our type.

It's not you, it's us, but actually, of course, it really is you.

Look, you've got to move on and find journals where your poems are appreciated, journals who publish them and then look forward to publishing more of them, where editors delight when your email lands in their inbox.

Sadly, we are on the verge of considering your persistence a form of harassment, and if we receive another submission from you, we will have to consider our legal options.

Jadedly yours,

Jonathon Gill, Poetry Editor.

Dear Mr. Leonard,

As an editor of another celebrated journal, you'll understand the fact that sometimes technically strong poems receive rejection notices. I'm sure you'll chuckle knowingly at this, but for no apparent reason, I've taken a bit of a dislike to you. This happens sometimes. They'll be published elsewhere, I have no doubt about it, but for a reason I couldn't manage to put my finger on, I felt myself gradually despising you as I read through them. I wouldn't take it at all personally, but your poems will not feature in the pages of *Acuity* while I am serving as editor.

Incidentally, I am contracted to edit another three issues.

Candidly yours,

Eloise Franklyn, Editor.

Dear Ms. Reiner,

It clearly states on our website that we publish poems in English from around the world but that we insist on the Anglican spelling of words. It is *our* language, after all, and how dare you, and by you I mean America, think you can abuse your independence by making up new ways to spell words just because you feel like it.

Send your American poems, but do keep in mind we will always deem 'color, 'humor', 'realize' and 'jewelry' all very grievous misspellings and we will be forced to question your ability to edit and proofread your work.

Please wait three months before submitting again to *Tea & Crumpet.*

Kind regards,

Austin Fairfax, Founder and Editor.

Dear Ms. Chesterton,

Thank you for sending us your poems, but we failed to see the relevance of including provocative pictures of yourself looking deep in thought during the writing of them. The downward camera angles in the photographs certainly allow for the exhibition of a great depth of cleavage, but that only served to accentuate the compensatory aspect of the pictures. The great swells of breast and resulting canyon only made the lacking depth of the poems more glaring.

Perhaps you misjudged the work we do here at *Squeeze Magazine*, but I wanted to be clear that we judge poem submissions solely on their literary qualities, and no advantage is given to would-be contributors of a seemingly more marketable image.

We couldn't accept any of these poems for publication in such an esteemed journal as ours, but we would discuss including your picture in a poetry calendar we are hoping to compile soon. This is one of several initiatives in the pipeline to show audiences just how sexy poetry can be. We were initially planning to limit ourselves to actual contributors to the journal, but on closer look found that, in cosmetic terms, our typical contributors just didn't quite match our vision of how sexy poetry can be.

If this is something that interests you please let us know, and we will send you a contract outlining our terms and conditions.

Most gratefully,

Dirk Freeman, Poetry and Visual Editor.

Dear Mr. Shakespeare,

Allow me, first of all, to sympathise. That name must be a terrible burden for you. It produced such high expectations in me, of course, and perhaps inevitably, these were expectations your poems fell short of rather spectacularly, and really, how could it be otherwise?

If it is consolation at all, were you to go by a more unassuming name, I expect the outcome would be no different.

Sympathetically,

Hailey Bloom, Associate Editor.

Speeding Quatrain

Dear Mr. Maxwell,

It is a narrow miss for you in your submission to *Scope*. It's also breakfast time and, if I'm honest, I'm harshest at this time of the day. I didn't sleep well at all. I feel like I'm forgetting something I must do, and I've over-cooked my eggs.

There's a good chance I'd have published one or two of these if I'd read them at another time of the day, but that's life, isn't it?

I wish you the best of luck placing them elsewhere, of course. Subscribe to our newsletter, or don't, whatever you like. I sometimes think I should put a desperate cry for help in the newsletter just to see if anyone actually looks at it.

Moodily yours,

Clarence Jervis, Prose and Poetry Associate.

Dear Ms. Harlow,

Terrible things have been reported in the news today, both at national and international level, and allow me to say congratulations on your name not being mentioned, and the likelihood that you remain currently safe from atrocity.

In Ireland a man has been jailed for running over his father-in-law and killing him at a family christening party, and I'm sure this very moment you're feeling great relief for the fact that you have not been knocked down and killed, assuming, of course, that you haven't been. It is unlikely, but I'd be awfully embarrassed if it turned out you were.

In Australia a man has died after being bitten by a highly venomous snake. He was trying to remove it from a childcare centre, can you believe it? It happened, so if you don't believe it, you only have to do a quick Google search and you'll see. From your biographical note I can see you live in Ireland, so I bet you're feeling quite thankful to St. Patrick right now for being as insistent as he was about their leaving.

Anyway, you're probably wondering why I'm telling you awful things from the news today. It's what we do here at *Blood Orange Moon Review* when we must turn poems down for publication. We like to think that notice of a failed submission of poems will seem less deflating when considered against the worse things that might have happened to you today. It would be bad form from you, in fact, to feel bad for yourself right now, when you ought to be thinking of the people who *really* suffered today.

While we will not publish your poems on this occasion, we certainly hope you will not be decapitated in a freak construction accident, or gunned down in a case of mistaken identity, or any other such tragedy.

Most sincerely,

Marianne Bryson, Reviews and Poetry.

Dear Mr. Patel,

Thank you for sending us these poems, which I will have to reject, on the basis that it is clearly stated we are a journal that only publishes women. The name *Gyno Poetry* is a statement of intent and also a pun on 'no guy', but we do regret it if we have been misleading in our aims. Your strongly stated claim to having valuable insight into female issues and experiences, sadly, does not affect this policy. I'll have to assume you possess a penis, and so you'll just have to send these poems elsewhere.

All best wishes,

Harriet Knight, Poetry Reader and Social Media Manager.

Dear Ms. Ormond,

Thank you for sending us these poems, which I regret to say we shall not be publishing.

In subject matter, we found them brash and dangerously liberal, particularly in their vision of gender equality, which our conservative journal has steadfastly opposed.

Perhaps you were ill-informed about the magazine. Anyway, I'll leave it at that, so you can get back to preparing Mr. Ormond's dinner and doing the ironing and such.

Manfully yours,

Frank Conroy, Editor and Illustrator.

Hush, Woman: A Magazine of Women's Poetry

Dear Mr. Hindley,

Your submission of poems has caught me in a bad moment. My wife demanded a divorce just this morning, and in so doing dropped a few choice remarks about my struggle with erectile dysfunction and the failures of the blue pill to rectify the matter.

Still, I have resolved to be an objective poetry editor, as in my critical capacity I am functioning very well, and I'm quite sure these outside factors in my life have had no bearing on my decision not to publish your poetry in an upcoming edition of *Swinging Pendulum*.

I expect you'll be rather disappointed with the outcome, but there are ways to release frustration that are not available to me but that I hope are to you.

Flaccidly yours,

Quentin Claiborne, Founding Editor.

Dear Ms. Carpenter,

I was more than a little mystified at your assemblage of these poems using words cut out from newspaper and magazine headlines. I've seen this practice in films and TV shows, but it is usually for communication from a criminal. It typically involves a death threat, blackmail or ransom of some sort. Your submission doesn't seem to be any of these things. Based on what I read, there seemed to be poetry with only rather law-abiding themes and topics. Perhaps you had a surplus of magazines and were out of ink for the printer. Perhaps it is simply a gimmick of yours. I would advise you to discontinue the practice, however, as it became somewhat of a distraction, one for which I must decline the chance to publish any of these in *Gaping Stanza*.

All best wishes,

Hilda Perez, Poetry Editor.

Dear Mr. Winkle,

I won't be able to publish your poems in the foreseeable future, but let me assure you, the decision is not a reflection of their quality. Please, do take the time to understand my reasons, which I'm happy to explain now in this letter.

I have recently been made single against my wishes, and I am not what you might call an eligible bachelor. I am not a catch. When I quipped once about having a face only a mother could love, I was quickly corrected, and by my mother no less, which was quite the setback for my self-esteem.

I'm the wrong side of fifty now, bald and persisting with an embarrassing comb-over. Once-severe acne has left my face unmercifully scarred and puckered. I have an unsightly paunch, scrawny legs and arms, a hunched back, and there is a musty smell that attached itself to me in my late twenties that I've never been able to escape or understand the source of.

I have no money and live in a bedsit more accurately described as a cocoon of mildew, so there is little in my life that women might deem attractive or alluring.

Still, I must work with what I've got, and therefore I have decided that I'll be giving priority to female would-be contributors, and I expect that until I am attached once more, there will be little room at *Clean Slate* for male-written poetry.

The plan is to prefer female poets and then, at the launches of its editions, make my availability known to them and, with any luck, stir up an option or two. It has been my experience that some female poets can be a lonely sort (something I'm hoping is still the case). I don't plan to be discriminating. It is a luxury I cannot afford. Female status and a heartbeat will suffice now.

I hope to get back to publishing poems by men very soon, naturally, and when I do, I'll be only delighted to consider your work.

Rather desperately,

Peter Helmer, Editor and Creative Director.

Dear Ms. Larmour,

Wow, these are very serious poems, aren't they? Here at *Enlightened Verse*, we do like to keep things a little less heavy. Perhaps you were misinformed about our aims. I think you'll find there are more than enough journals out there for poems that take themselves far too seriously.

I can't publish any of these, naturally. For starters, there isn't a rhyme to be found in one of them. We enjoy happy, playful, rhythmic rhyming, which you'd know if you'd read our back catalogue, which is available from our website.

My good mood is entirely shattered now, too, after reading your six pages of misery. I'm about to eat a large bowl of chocolate ice-cream in the hope I can recover it.

Optimistically yours,

Katherine Wren, Editor-in-Chief.

Dear Mr. Fenton,

Firstly, happy birthday! I hope you had a great day and received a lovely big cake and great presents. Your suggestion, however, that *Mixed Fortune Review* should publish your poems as a birthday present to you is not something we can do. Other editors might be so generous, but I am not very much into birthday festivities ever since I turned eight and was emotionally scarred by a hired clown who started me on a long and expensive path of never-ending therapy.

Anyway, I do wish you great success in your writing, and hope you will see these poems published elsewhere sometime soon.

Always graciously,

Cliona Hesham, Founder and Poetry Editor.

Dear Ms. Barnes,

I'm sorry that you are disappointed about the success rate of your submissions to *Wind Gap*, but I am going to have to turn down this batch as well.

I hope that when you do have work published by us, it will have been worth it. We depend on the submissions we receive, and they all – published and unpublished – drive the quality of the journal.

It was not necessary to include a list of previous contributors to *Wind Gap* whose work you believe is, in general, of a lesser quality than your own. You may be right, but we make the best judgement we can with the poems we are sent.

I would say that focusing on those poets and questioning their credentials is not the most helpful approach.

Perhaps it would be better to spend more time analysing the kind of work we have published and considering it in terms of our ethos, which you'll find on our website. You may have already written the poem we'd love to publish, and maybe you just haven't thought to send us that one yet.

Kindest regards,

Miranda Link, Associate Editor and Website Manager.

Dear Mr. Miller,

You have some nerve sending poems to *Valium Literary Journal* for consideration. I'll not be reading these, and I even thought to bin them without response, but my seething has got the better of me so here I am responding.

We met at a literary festival a few years ago and had several drinks and a lively chat about the Romantic poets, and in the process built up a decent tab. You went to the bathroom and that was the last I saw of you.

You must have slipped out, leaving me with the bill, which I paid with the last of my money before walking back to my hotel in the teeming rain because I couldn't cover a cab fare.

I understand poets are a selfish species, but I never understood the depths they might stoop to until my encounter with you.

Don't send your work again to any journal or anthology at which I am editor. I am only sorry that I cannot serve as editor at all of them so that I can make sure you are never published again.

Hatefully yours,

Jesse Potter, Managing Director.

Dear Mr. Allenby,

I am aware that I once thanked you for sending your poems to us, and that I urged you to send more. It isn't that I was being insincere then. No, I totally meant it at the time. It's just that several submissions later, I regret what I said. I want to take it back, if you wouldn't mind.

I wish you'd never sent poems our way. I wish I'd known it then and told you, but I didn't know it, and I think it was correct to give you encouragement, and to believe that you might improve your writing.

I'm ready, at last, to be entirely honest with you. I don't want to see your poetry ever again.

If it hasn't already been made clear, I'll finish by saying I'm not going to publish these poems. They are not exceptionally bad, I expect, but then I find it difficult to assess them objectively as there has been an accumulative effect of having read many submissions from you.

Reading poems from you has become just like a persistent itch I needed to not scratch in the beginning but kept scratching and scratching until it became a raw and fizzing infection.

Every good wish,

Brenda Connolly, Poetry and Reviews Editor.

Loose Goose Poetry

Dear Ms. Keating,

It's quite hilarious how you think that following me on all my social media is going to make me want to publish your poetry at *Trident*. How original of you! I mean, you're the first person who has ever thought of that. Wow!

I hope you appreciate irony, because had you not pulled that cynical little stunt, I think I would have used two of these poems. You can consider yourself black-balled now, of course.

Spitefully,

Walter Talbot, Editor and Graphic Design.

Thanks

I would like to thank Truth Serum Press for believing in this manuscript, and to thank Matt Potter for the hard work done during design and editing.

I would like to thank whichever poet wrote the Facebook rant that inspired it – I honestly cannot remember who it was, though I probably shouldn't name him anyway (of course it was a man). I would like to thank, most sincerely, all the editors who both published and rejected my work over the years. You provided all the material, so your contribution is huge. I hope editors particularly enjoy this (albeit unusual) acknowledgement of their often-unacknowledged work.

Edward O'Dwyer was born in Limerick, Ireland, in 1984, where he currently lives and works as a secondary school teacher.

To date, he has written three collections of poetry, all from Salmon Poetry – *The Rain on Cruise's Street* (2014), *Bad News, Good News, Bad News* (2017) and *Exquisite Prisons* (2022).

He has also published two collections of short fiction – the micro fiction collection *Cheat Sheets* (Truth Serum Press, 2018), and *The Man Who Became Poems and Other Stories* (Limerick Writers' Centre, 2023).

O'Dwyer's work has featured in many journals and anthologies worldwide, including *The Forward Book of Poetry*, and has been nominated regularly for Forward, Pushcart and Best of the Web prizes. 'The Whole History of Dancing' won the 'Best Single Poem' award at the Eigse Michael Hartnett Festival in 2018.

He has been selected by Poetry Ireland for their Introductions Series and shortlisted for a Hennessy Award for 'Emerging Poetry', and in 2021 was appointed Poet Laureate of Adare, Co. Limerick, as part of their Poetry Town initiative.

O'Dwyer has also edited two anthologies of poetry for Limerick community publisher Revival Press – *Sextet* (2010) and *Sextet 2* (2016).

Also by Edward O'Dwyer
from Truth Serum Press

truthserumpress.net/catalogue/fiction/cheat-sheets/

978-1-925536-60-7 (paperback)
978-1-925536-61-4 (eBook)

praise for Cheat Sheets

"These are shards that insist on being read, and then read again."
Alan McMonagle, author of *Psychotic Episodes*

"These are wicked little gems!"
Donal Ryan, author of *The Spinning Heart*

"A side-splitting study on the absurdity of human behaviour."
Tanya Farrelly, author of *The Girl Behind the Lens*

Also from TRUTH SERUM PRESS

truthserumpress.net/catalogue/

 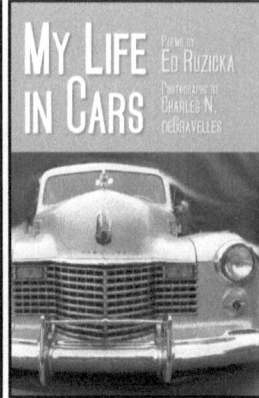 

- *The Crazed Wind* by Nod Ghosh
  978-1-925536-58-4 (paperback) 978-1-925536-59-1 (eBook)
- *My Life in Cars* by Ed Ruzicka
  978-1-922427-10-6 (paperback) 978-1-922427-11-3 (eBook)
- *The Story of the Milkman* by Alan Walowitz
  978-1-925536-76-8 (paperback) 978-1-925536-77-5 (eBook)

- *On the Bitch* by Matt Potter
  978-1-925536-45-4 (paperback) 978-1-925536-46-1 (eBook)
- *Decennia* by Jan Chronister
  978-1-925536-98-0 (paperback) 978-1-925536-99-7 (eBook)
- *Dollhouse Masquerade* by Samuel E. Cole
  978-1-925536-21-8 (paperback) 978-1-925536-22-5 (eBook)

www.ingramcontent.com/pod-product-compliance
Lightning Source LLC
Chambersburg PA
CBHW030347180626
46812CB00007B/2789